To my children:
Cal, Eoin, Davy, Katherine and Rory, and
especially Eoin whose original dreams, aged
three, inspired the writing of this story…
G.B.

Adam and Pingu, with all my love
F.H.

First published 2018 by Walker Books Ltd
87 Vauxhall Walk, London SE11 5HJ

2 4 6 8 10 9 7 5 3 1

Text © 2018 Gerry Byrne
Illustrations © 2018 Faye Hanson

The right of Gerry Byrne and Faye Hanson to be identified as author and
illustrator respectively of this work has been asserted by them in accordance with
the Copyright, Designs and Patents Act 1988

This book has been typeset in Alice

Printed in China

British Library Cataloguing in Publication Data:
a catalogue record for this book is available from the British Library

ISBN 978-1-4063-2325-2

www.walker.co.uk

WALKER BOOKS
AND SUBSIDIARIES
LONDON • BOSTON • SYDNEY • AUCKLAND

ALL AT SEA

Gerry Byrne

Illustrated by
Faye Hanson

One day, Liam's mammy and daddy came home with
a present for Liam, a present for his big sister Mary
and a new baby brother for them both.

Liam opened his present and out came a mammy hippo,
a daddy hippo, two little hippos and a tiny, baby hippo.

Liam played with them all day, and Mary
played with her building blocks.

That night Liam put his hippo family
– the mammy hippo, the daddy hippo and
the two little hippos – beside his bed so that
he could see them and they could see him.
"I thought there were three little hippos," said Mammy.

"No," said Liam. "Only two."

"Are you sure?" asked Mammy, holding up a crocodile
with the baby hippo sticking out of its mouth.
"What about this baby hippo?"
"Oh!" said Liam. "That baby hippo got lost and the big crocodile
with enormous teeth gobbled him all up –

SNAP! CRUNCH! GULP!

"Poor Baby Hippo," sighed Mammy.
"Night-night. Sleep tight. Don't
let the bedbugs bite."

But Liam didn't sleep tight.

He had a bad dream.

PITTER-PATTER,
PITTER-PATTER, PITTER-PATTER
went Liam's little feet as he ran into Mammy and Daddy's room.

"I had a bad dream," he said as he climbed into bed
and squeezed in between them. Mammy and Daddy
cuddled him, the baby mumbled and Liam
tumbled into a deep, deep sleep.

The next night Liam put his hippo family – the
mammy and the daddy and the two little hippos – beside
his bed so that he could see them and they could see him.
"I wonder where Baby Hippo has got to tonight?" said Mammy.
"Is that him, underneath the elephant?" she asked.

SQUASH! SCRUNCH! SQUELCH!

said Liam, "Baby Hippo got lost and the elephant was
stomping along and he thought Baby Hippo was just
a piece of poo and he stood on him!"

"Poor Baby Hippo," sighed Mammy. "Night-night. Sleep tight."

Mammy didn't say anything about bedbugs this time

But Liam didn't sleep tight.

He had a bad dream.

PITTER-PATTER,
PITTER-PATTER, PITTER-PATTER
went Liam's little feet as he ran into Mammy and Daddy's room.

He squeezed in between them
and said, "I had another bad dream."
Mammy gave him a cuddle, Daddy's snoring rumbled,
the baby mumbled and Liam tumbled into sleep.

The next night Liam put his hippo family – the mammy
and the daddy and the two little hippos – beside his bed
so that he could see them and they could see him.

"I wonder where Baby Hippo has got to tonight?" asked Mammy.

"I don't know," said Liam.

"Mammy!" shouted Mary. "I can't use the loo."

"Yes you can," said Mammy.

"NO I CAN'T!" shouted Mary.

"And why not?" asked Mammy.

"Because there's a hippo
  in the toilet."

SPLASH! SPLOSH! SPLISH!

said Liam. "The hippos went for a swim and Baby Hippo got lost and then he got swept over the waterfall –

SPLASH! SPLOSH! SPLISH!

"Poor Baby Hippo," sighed Mammy.

"Night-night."

But Liam didn't sleep tight.

He had a bad dream.

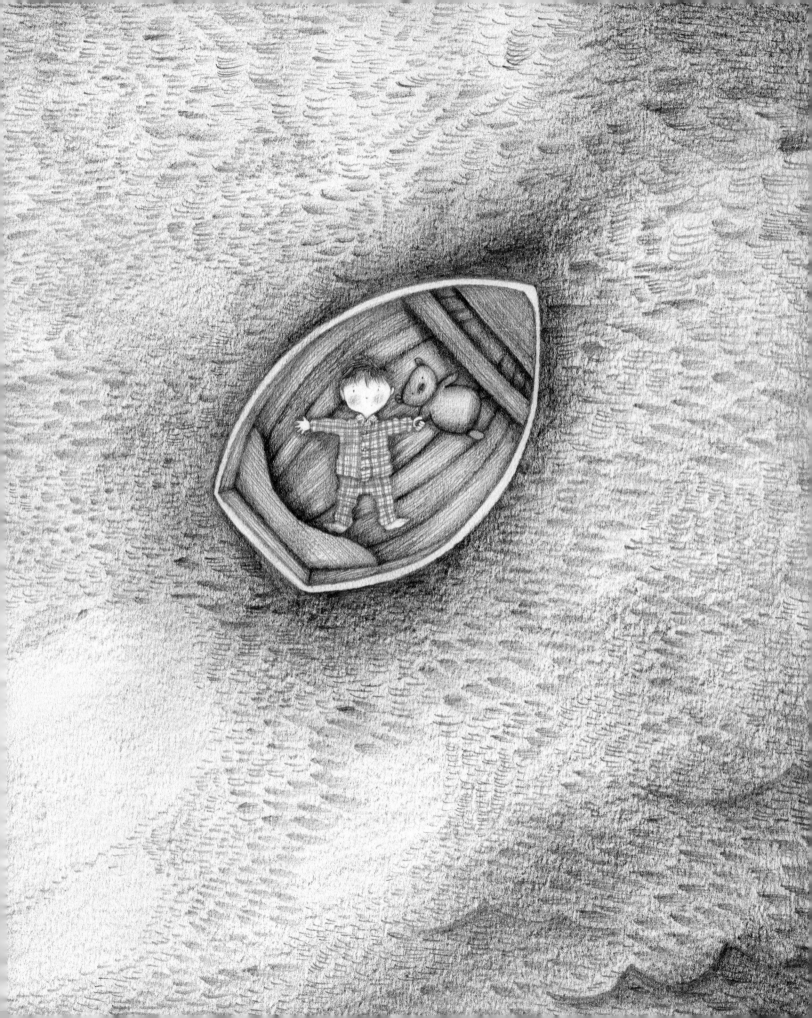

PITTER-PATTER,
PITTER-PATTER, PITTER-PATTER
went Liam's little feet as he ran into Mammy and Daddy's room.

He squeezed in between them
and said, "I had another bad dream."
Mammy grumbled, Daddy's tummy rumbled, the baby
mumbled but Liam couldn't get back to sleep.

Liam sat up. "I've got to find Baby Hippo!"

He looked in the crocodile's
mouth. Not there!

He looked under the
elephant. Not there!

He looked down the toilet. Not there!
Baby Hippo was nowhere to be found.

Liam went back to Mammy and Daddy's bed.

The baby was in *his* place, between Mammy and Daddy – giggling! His baby brother smiled up at him, holding something tight in his tiny fist. Baby Brother opened his hand and there was Baby Hippo! Liam put his hand out to take it and as he did so Baby Brother caught hold of Liam's finger and put it in his mouth. It tickled.

Liam giggled,
the baby
giggled.

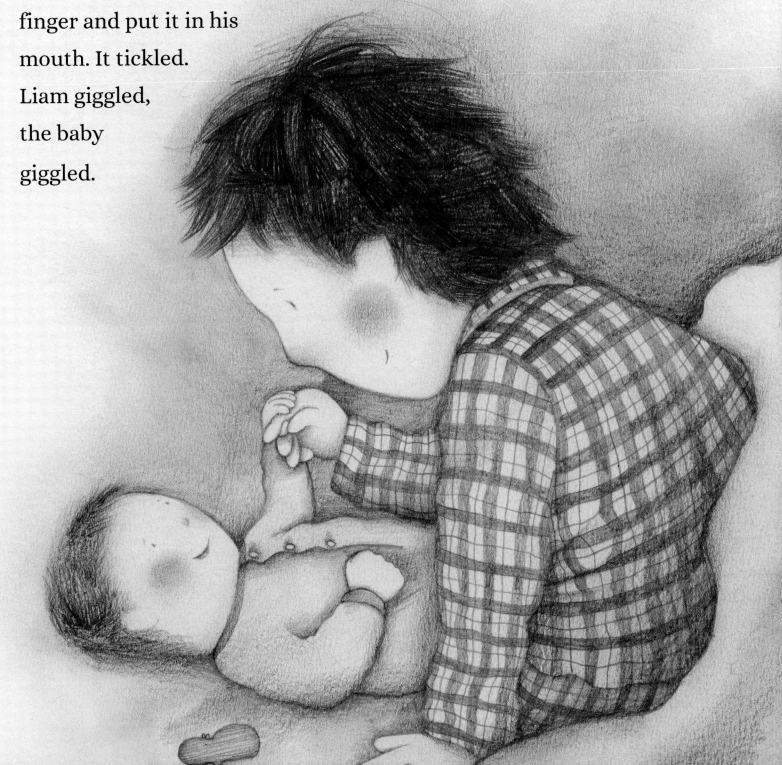

That night, before Mammy tucked him into bed, Liam put his hippo family – the mammy and the daddy and two little hippos *and* the baby hippo – beside his bed so that he could see them and they could see him.

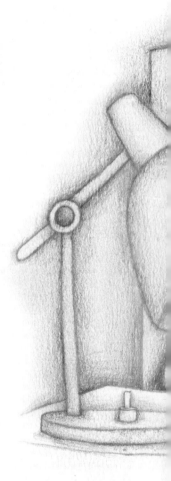

"I see Baby Hippo is back with his mammy and daddy and sister and brother," said Mammy.

"That's right", said Liam.

"Oh good," said Mammy. "Night-night. Sleep tight. Don't let the bedbugs bite."

That night Liam slept tight.